A DANCE LIKE STARLIGHT

One Ballerina's Dream

BY **KRISTY DEMPSEY**

ILLUSTRATED BY **FLOYD COOPER**

Philomel Books AN IMPRINT OF PENGUIN GROUP (USA)

For my mama, who dreamed every dream
I ever had right along with me.   —K.D.

For Deanna, Teyanna and Brianna.   —F.C.

Stars hardly shine in the New York City sky,
with the factories spilling out
pillars of smoke
and streetlights spreading
bright halos round their pin-top faces.
It makes it hard to find a star,

even harder to make a wish,
the one wish that
if I could just breathe it out loud
to the first star of night,
I might be able to believe it true.

Every evening, I search the sky
while Mama unpins the extra wash
she's taken on to make ends meet.
From our rooftop, I gaze at the city skyline
and whisper my wish even though
there are no stars to be found,
not a single one
night after night after night.

Mama says wishing on stars is a waste anyhow,
says you don't need stars in the sky
to make your dreams come true.
Hope can pick your dream up, she says,
off the floor of your heart,
when you think it can't happen,
no how, no way,
    though unlike wishing
    Mama says
    hoping
    is hard work.

If there's one thing Mama knows,
    it's hard work.
Mama works all day long every day,
and most times on into the night,
for the ballet school.
She's been cleaning and stitching
    costumes there
since before I was a baby.

Through the years,
we've spent so much time around ballet
for fittings
and rehearsals
and mending
that before I even knew it
a dream got inside my heart.
I didn't have to tell Mama for her
        to take notice.
She saw my dreaming when I tiptoed
        to her sewing corner
to slip on those beautiful costumes.
She saw it when I twirled in front of her faded mirror,
repeating every move I'd seen at their rehearsals.

The Ballet Master saw, too,
when I stood backstage during a recital
and did an entire dance in the wings,
from beginning to final bow.

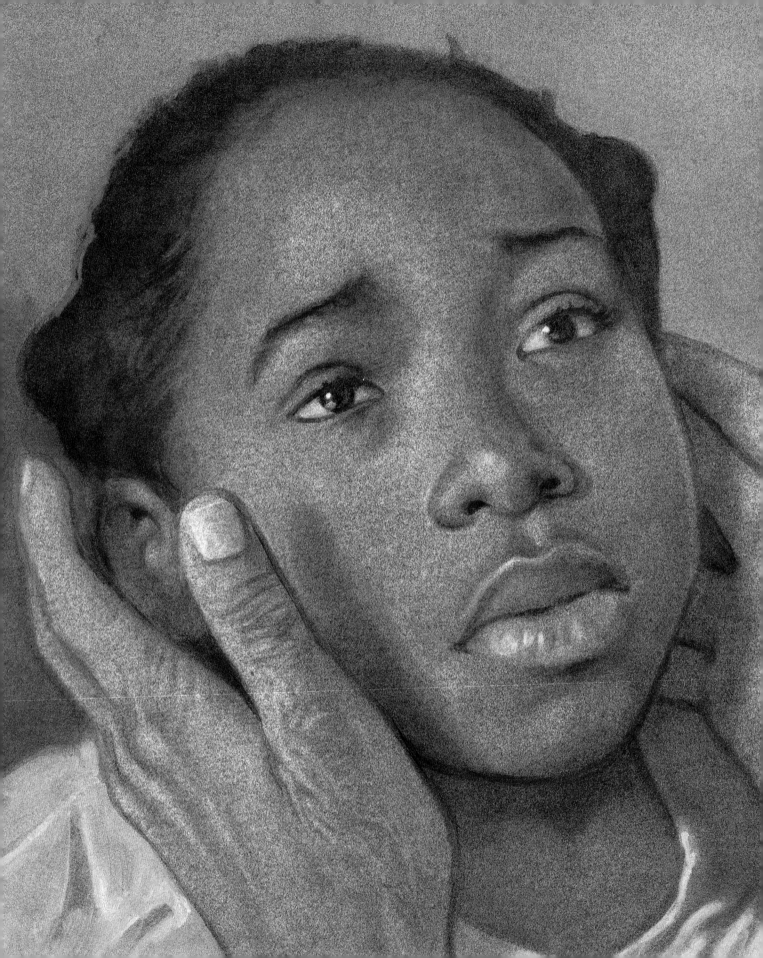

I turned away
when I saw him watching,
ashamed how he saw me
trying to do their dance.
But he took my face in his hands
and looked into my eyes.
"Brava, *ma petite*," he told me. "Brava."
That's when hope picked my dream up
from the floor of my heart,
just like Mama said,
and it started growing.

The Ballet Master made an arrangement
for me to join lessons each day
from the back of the room,
even though I can't perform
onstage with white girls.
Every class I try harder
to stand taller,
to leap higher,
to dance better.

And every once in a while,
when Mrs. Adams is especially surprised
or perhaps even pleased with my form,
she asks me to demonstrate a movement
            for the whole class.
With every bend, I hope.
With every plié,
every turn,
every grand jeté, I hope.
The harder I work, the bigger
            my hope grows,
and the more I wonder:
Could a colored girl like me
ever become
a prima ballerina?

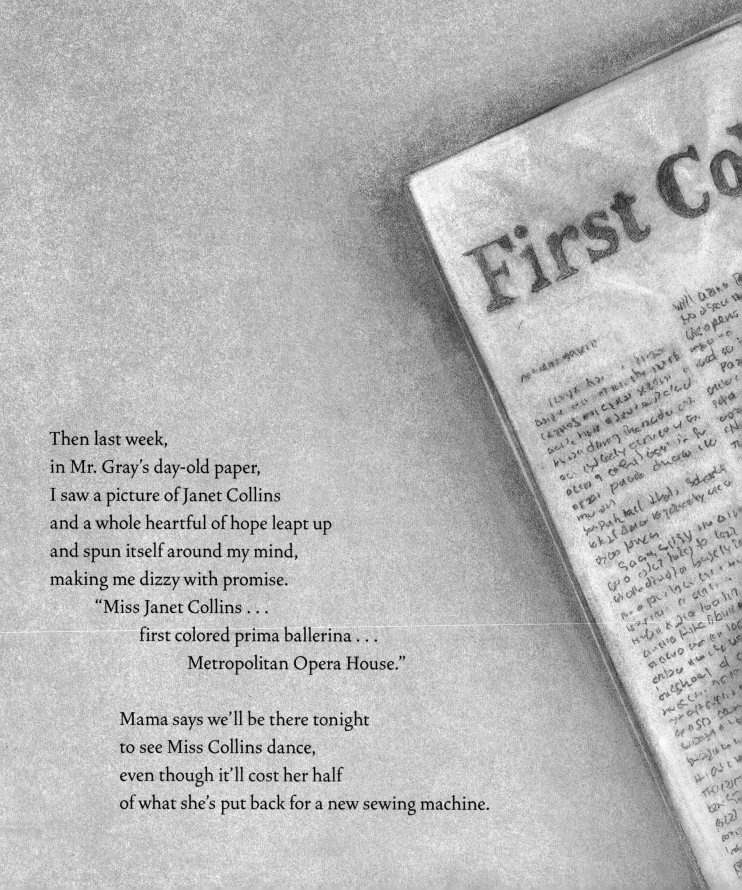

Then last week,
in Mr. Gray's day-old paper,
I saw a picture of Janet Collins
and a whole heartful of hope leapt up
and spun itself around my mind,
making me dizzy with promise.
  "Miss Janet Collins . . .
        first colored prima ballerina . . .
            Metropolitan Opera House."

Mama says we'll be there tonight
to see Miss Collins dance,
even though it'll cost her half
of what she's put back for a new sewing machine.

Waiting now
for the bus,
my feet won't stop
their tippy-tappy,
jumpin' jiggle,
can't-hardly-wait wiggle.

It takes
  three
    different
        buses
to get where we're going.
I keep checking Mama's watch
and straining my neck to see how far we've gone.
But in this crowded bus from our place in the back
all I can see are sidewalks and storefronts.
It makes it hard to see the tops of high-rises,
landmarks that would let me know we're close,
ones I would recognize
from wishing on a skyline every single night.

When we finally reach our stop,
I hop from the bus
and stare
at the huge building in front of me.
I watch fancy people entering through the doorway.
I tug my jacket
and smooth my hair,
        then Mama takes my hand and we go inside.

        As we enter the auditorium of
        the Metropolitan Opera House,
        I think
        I must look small.
                Even Mama looks small.

The curtain goes up and
I inch forward to the edge of my seat,
listening to the rush of music
and the round voices of the singers,
but waiting, watching for Miss Collins.

When she glides onto the stage,
I don't know
if I am dreaming,
if I am even breathing,
because she doesn't seem to touch the floor.
She twirls and
my heart jumps up from where I'm sitting,
soaring, dancing,
opening wide with the swell of music.

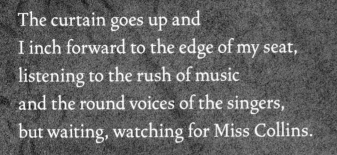

In my heart I'm the one leaping
       across that stage,
raising myself high on those shoulders,
then falling
       slowly
              slowly
                     slowly
                            to the arms below.

              It's like Miss Collins is dancing for me,
              only for me,
              showing me who I can be.
                     All my hoping
                            wells up and spills over,
                                   dripping all my dreams onto my Sunday dress.

When it's all over,
I clap for the singers,
the members of the chorus,
for the musicians
and the maestro.
But I shout for Janet Collins,
joining a chorus
of "Brava, brava,"
many voices strong.

Hope
puffs up my chest
just a bit.
One day,
those voices
will be
for me.

Mama and I dance our way home
under the night sky,
and I don't even try
to catch a glimpse
of the first star.
No need to waste my wishes.
I've got dreams coming true.

AUTHOR'S NOTE

On November 13, 1951, four years before singer Marian Anderson's Metropolitan Opera debut, dancer Janet Collins became the first African American hired to perform under contract with the Metropolitan Opera. Though she had been denied the opportunity to dance with other ballet troupes because of the color of her skin, Met Ballet Master Zachary Solov was so taken with her skill and beauty as a dancer, his choreography of the opening night opera was inspired by her movement. Rudolf Bing, general manager of the Met from 1950 to 1972, considered his greatest achievement to be having hired Miss Collins, breaking the barrier that existed for African American performers of the era.

Miss Collins's performance on opening night and the fact that she was "colored," as African Americans were called at that time, were both highly publicized in advance. Though I have only imagined this little girl and her mother were at the Met to see Miss Collins perform, I hope many women, regardless of their age or the color of their skin, are inspired to achieve their own dreams through her historic performance.

PHILOMEL BOOKS Published by the Penguin Group
Penguin Group (USA) LLC
375 Hudson Street, New York, NY 10014

USA | Canada | UK | Ireland | Australia | New Zealand | India | South Africa | China
penguin.com
A Penguin Random House Company

Text copyright © 2014 by Kristin Dempsey. Illustrations copyright © 2014 by Floyd Cooper.
Penguin supports copyright. Copyright fuels creativity, encourages diverse voices, promotes free speech, and creates a vibrant culture. Thank you for buying an authorized edition of this book and for complying with copyright laws by not reproducing, scanning, or distributing any part of it in any form without permission. You are supporting writers and allowing Penguin to continue to publish books for every reader.

Library of Congress Cataloging-in-Publication Data
Dempsey, Kristy. A dance like starlight : one ballerina's dream / Kristy Dempsey ; illustrated by Floyd Cooper. pages cm
Summary: A young girl growing up in Harlem in the 1950s, whose mother cleans and stitches costumes for a ballet company, dreams of becoming a prima ballerina one day, and is thrilled to see a performance of Janet Collins, the first "colored" prima ballerina.
[1. Ballet dancing—Fiction. 2. African Americans—Fiction. 3. Discrimination—Fiction. 4. Collins, Janet—Fiction. 5. New York (N.Y.)—History—1951—Fiction.] I. Cooper, Floyd, illustrator. II. Title. PZ7.D41136Dan 2014 [E]—dc23 2013009520
Manufactured in the United States Of America ISBN 978-0-399-25284-6
3 5 7 9 10 8 6 4

Edited by Jill Santopolo. Design by Amy Wu and Semadar Megged. Text set in 17.5-point Vendetta OT Medium.
Paintings were created using a subtractive process. The medium is mixed media.